The Amazing
ANIMAL
STORYBOOK

Written and illustrated by
ANNE and KEN McKIE

TREASURE PRESS

•THE ELEPHANT•
in the Paper Bag

There was once an elephant who lived in a great big park with lots of other animals. Although he was very happy there he longed to see the world outside. 'Don't you go outside!' cried the other elephants. 'You might get lost.'

'I'll ask the giraffes what is outside the park gates,' he thought to himself. 'As they are the tallest animals in the world and can see over the gates – they must know.' But the giraffes told him not to be so nosey.

Next he asked the squirrels that jumped about on the tops of the trees, but they said they were too shy to look over the park gates. 'I must go outside,' said the elephant. 'But what shall I do if anyone sees me? Where shall I hide, as I am rather big.'

The squirrels had the answer. 'When we feel shy and want to hide, we pop into a paper bag. No one ever thinks of looking inside.' And they kindly gave him the biggest one they had.

Mrs. Griffin
sept. 1990

First published in Great Britain in 1986 in
four separate volumes by
The Hamlyn Publishing Group Limited
This edition published in 1989 by
Treasure Press
Michelin House
81 Fulham Road
London SW3 6RB

ISBN 1-85051 443 7

Printed in Hong Kong

Off went the elephant with the paper bag perched on his trunk. At the park gates he hid among some tall pine trees. His legs blended in with their tall trunks. 'Look!' gasped one of the keepers, 'there's a paper bag in that tree. How did it get up there?' He fetched a ladder, climbed up and snatched it off the elephant's trunk.

The keeper never even noticed the elephant. He opened the park gates and threw the bag in the bin outside. 'I will not have litter in my nice clean park,' he muttered. Meanwhile the elephant crept out of the park unnoticed.

'The squirrels were right,' giggled the elephant. 'Hiding in a paper bag really works. The keeper didn't see me at all.' So he picked the bag out of the bin and went off down the road.

Suddenly a car pulled up very close to him. 'Oh dear!' gasped the elephant holding on to his paper bag. The two people in the front didn't notice him at all. But a little boy peering out of the sun-roof did.
'Look! There's an elephant wearing a paper bag!' he shrieked.
'Now don't tell such stories, or you'll not go to the park to see the animals,' his mother said crossly. The elephant just shook with laughter.

17

He walked on until he came to a house. Three men were sitting on the roof mending the tiles. The elephant crept past on tiptoe. He was sure they would see him. One of the men rubbed his eyes. 'There's an elephant,' he gasped, 'and he's carrying a paper bag.'

'I expect he's brought your sandwiches,' joked the other two men. They laughed so much they almost fell off the roof.

Next the elephant passed a block of flats. His head just came level with the second floor window. He could see twin boys sitting in their highchairs eating their lunch.

'Ele . . .' screamed one child.

'. . . phant,' yelled the other.

But all their mother could see was the bag hanging on the elephant's tail as he walked by. She went wild with delight. 'You said your first word boys! But it wasn't an elephant . . . it was a PAPER BAG!'

The elephant walked past shops and offices. It was lunchtime and everyone was so busy they never even noticed him. As he strolled past one office window, a lady dropped her apple-core into his bag . . . and carried on typing!

Poor elephant. He began to feel quite lonely. Hardly anyone had noticed him. 'It's because I've been hiding in this paper bag,' he said to himself. 'The squirrels were right. It really does work.'

As he turned the corner, he stepped into the city square which was full of people and television cameras. The television crew were standing round the fountain interviewing the Mayor for the evening news.

24

'Great,' thought the elephant. 'Now's my chance to get on television.' Quickly he pushed and nudged his way to the front. Can you believe it? Not one person noticed him.

'It's this paper bag,' cried the elephant, 'I'll not hide in it anymore. I'm going to throw it away.'

He gave one great blow down his trunk, and the bag blew right in to the television reporter's face.

The reporter grabbed the cameraman, who grabbed the man with the lights . . .
And the whole television crew fell, SPLASH, into the fountain, and every bit of the recording was ruined.

'There will be no television news tonight,' shouted the onlookers. So they all rushed home to see what would happen instead.
'Time I went home too,' said the elephant, running through the streets unnoticed.

He reached the park quite out of breath. The gates were wide open. The keepers were nowhere to be seen. The elephant tiptoed up to their little hut.

They were sitting watching an empty television screen.

"There will be no T·V· News
tonight. All because of a paper bag!
A strong gust of wind blew it into
our interviewer's face. The whole
T·V· crew fell into the fountain and
all the film got wet. Instead of the
news this evening, we are going to
show you a very old film, in black
and white – all about ELEPHANTS."

33

The elephant rushed off to tell the squirrels about his adventures beyond the park gates. 'I think I might ask for another one of your paper bags one fine day,' said the elephant with a grin.

•THE DOG•
that Glowed in the Dark

Daly was puzzled. He could tell something secret was going on. Several times the children came in with packages and rushed upstairs with them right away.

If Daly listened outside their bedroom door, he could hear paper rustling and lots of giggling and laughing. This went on for weeks.

One day he followed them to a store to find out what they were buying. But a big notice on the window said 'No Dogs Allowed' so he had to stay outside.

He looked everywhere, until one glorious day he found what he was looking for!

All the children were at school. Daly was kicking the closet (because he thought it was locked). When all of a sudden the door opened very slowly . . .

. . . and out fell a skeleton! — followed by lots of other things. And they all fell right on top of Daly. 'Fancy-dress costumes!' cried Daly. 'They've been buying fancy-dress costumes.'

'And masks and wigs and mustaches and make-up!'

Daly was sitting quietly pretending to read when the children came home from school. 'We are going to give you a surprise tonight,' the children said to Daly. 'I shall look forward to that,' thought Daly to himself.

It took them a long time, but at last the children were ready. 'Very nice,' nodded Daly. 'But a little bit ordinary!'
The children gasped. 'Ordinary!' they all cried together. 'We've been saving up for weeks to buy these costumes.'

Daly picked up the box of make-up and climbed up on a stool. 'How about this and this and this and last of all this. Now that's what I call different.'

'I think I would make a very good make-up artist on television or in the movies,'
Daly said in his grandest voice. 'Who ever heard of a dog doing make-up?'
shrieked the children.

Later that night, the children were going out to see a movie about monsters.
'Come with us, Daly,' they teased, 'and you can see how to make up a monster.'

Poor Daly stomped up the stairs in a temper. 'I'll have another look in their make-up box,' he thought to himself. And he took the box out of the closet.

'Well, look what I've found,' sniggered Daly. 'This invisible make-up glows in the dark.' Quickly he made his face up and reached for the light switch.

'Help!' screamed Daly, when he switched off the bedroom light. 'I really do glow in the dark.'

Then Daly had an idea. A great big grin crept across his face. He ran round the children's bedroom, drawing all over the walls and drapes with the make-up stick.

As soon as he heard the children coming home from the movies, he jumped in the closet where he hid and waited.

The children were chattering about the monsters in the film. At last they jumped into bed. But when they switched out the light . . .

GIANT MONSTERS appeared round the walls and on the drapes. And worst of all, a little monster jumped out of the closet and ran round the bedroom.

Mommy came hurrying up the stairs and switched the light on. 'I can't see any monsters,' she said with a smile. 'It's only Daly.' And she patted the dog. 'I should never have let you go to see that movie about monsters,' she said.

It was Daly's turn to laugh now. He told them all about the make-up that glowed in the dark.

And how it worked with the bedroom light off.

Even Mommy had to laugh. 'Serves you all right for teasing poor Daly. I think he makes a wonderful make-up artist.' And the children had to agree.

Daly is kept very busy nowadays, making up monsters . . . SO WATCH OUT!

·THE ANTEATER·
with the Amazing Tongue

Sometimes, if they had been very good, Jilly and James could go to the store and choose some candy. It took them a long time to decide which ones to have — there were so many to choose from.

The storekeeper put the candy in two bags and gave Jilly and James one each. 'Try not to drop them on the ground,' he smiled. 'They will get dirty and not be fit to eat.'

Almost every time they had a bag of candy one would fall out and roll away.
Now both children knew that they should never pick up candy from the ground.

It was really hard to walk away and leave a candy just lying there. What a dreadful waste!

Jilly and James could remember every single candy that they had ever dropped, what sort it was, and exactly where they had dropped it.

'I wonder what happens to all the candy that children drop,' said James.
'If we can't pick them up, where do they go?'

73

Now one day in the garden, James dropped a candy on the grass. But when he looked down it had gone. That's very odd! How could a candy disappear just like that?

The children just had to find out what was happening to their candy. So they dropped a whole bag. Quick as a flash they vanished. Not one single candy was left!

All of a sudden Jilly remembered that she had some popcorn in the house. Quickly she scattered it all over the garden. Then both children hid behind the hedge.

The popcorn began to disappear at once. Then from behind a bush came a loud 'HICCUP'.
'It must be that worm,' gasped Jilly.

'A worm can't hiccup as loud as that,' said James. 'We'd better take a look behind the bush'... They were in for a shock! The strangest creature peered back at them. 'Are you a badger?' asked Jilly, very politely.

'I'm nothing of the kind,' laughed the strange creature. 'I am an ANTEATER,' and he hiccuped very loudly. 'Have you been eating too many ants?' asked Jilly. The Anteater pulled a face. 'Certainly not,' he said. 'I hate ants, nasty, tickling things.'

'I eat all the candy that children drop and are not allowed to pick up,' said the Anteater proudly. 'You see, I can reach them with my extra-long tongue.' At last the children knew where their candy had gone.

The Anteater's tongue was amazing. It could stretch across the lawn, over the hedge, and right into the garden next door. 'As a rule I only eat the candy that falls on the ground,' he said. 'But if some kind person were to offer me a candy I wouldn't say no.'

Jilly and James couldn't wait to tell their friends about the amazing Anteater. Soon the garden was full of children. And every one brought a different kind of candy. The Anteater loved them all, and soon he was full.

When he could not eat another candy, the Anteater said, 'Shall I show you some tricks with my long tongue? Watch! I can tie it in a knot, loop the loop, even tie it in a bow. I can do useful things too.

'See that apple tree over there,' said the Anteater. Quickly he put out his tongue until it reached right up into the branches. When the children looked up into the tree it was empty. The Anteater had picked every apple and dropped them into baskets.

'Dad will be pleased,' said James to Jilly.
'He hates picking apples.'

'Now, gather round children,' shouted the Anteater, who was really enjoying himself. 'Everyone has to hide something in the garden.' The Anteater closed his eyes tightly. 'I bet I can find every single thing without moving from this spot.'

The children ran all over the garden. They hid their hats and shoes and all sorts of other things. Jilly hid her socks, James hid his sandals, and the baby hid his hat.

When the children had finished, they gathered round the Anteater. 'Now close your eyes and count up to one hundred,' he told them. 'One, two, three, four...', counted the children as fast as they could.

The Anteater didn't move – he just put out his amazing tongue. It reached round the bushes and behind the flowers. It went through the watering can, into the wheelbarrow and under plant pots. 'Ready,' yelled the Anteater.

The children's eyes sprang open. 'But we've only counted up to six,' they gasped. And then they looked at the Anteater and just could not stop laughing. He had found their things, and was wearing them . . . all at once.

Now the very next day the Anteater followed Jilly and James to school. 'I'm afraid you will have to stay outside,' said Jilly. 'I don't think Anteaters go to school.'

So the Anteater stayed outside in the playground and peeked through the classroom window. He put his tongue out at the children but made sure the teacher did not see him.

'Today, children,' said the teacher, 'I am going to tell you about a very unusual animal.' And she pinned a picture up on the wall. 'IT'S AN ANTEATER,' yelled the children.

'That's amazing,' said the teacher. 'You all deserve a reward!' So she took a candy for everyone from her jar and put them on her desk. But when she turned round every candy had gone.

'You should never gobble your candy as quickly as that,' scolded the teacher. 'It wasn't us,' cried the children. 'It was the Anteater.'

'Oh, now really children!' said the teacher. 'Anteaters eat ants, that is why they are called ANTEATERS. Who ever heard of an anteater that eats candy?'

The children just smiled. They knew an Anteater who just loved to eat candy.

·THE CAT·
that Played the Flute

There was once a cat called Kilkenny. He lived in a little stone cottage with his Master and Mistress, in a place where the mountains reached down to the sea.

Now Kilkenny played the flute. He played so well that everybody from miles around came to listen and dance to his marvellous music.

Kilkenny loved to sit on the rocks near the sea and play his flute really loudly, as the waves crashed on to the shore. One morning he noticed the strangest man dressed all in black.

He was standing on the rocks waving his arms up and down. 'Oh dear!' thought Kilkenny, 'If he doesn't get off that rock soon he'll be cut off by the tide.'

'Hurry up sir!' yelled the cat, 'Or you'll drown.' The man held on to Kilkenny's flute and scrambled up the rocks to safety.

'You look just like a wet penguin,' giggled Kilkenny.
'I am a GREAT CONDUCTOR' said the man with a bow.
'Really!' replied the cat looking very interested. 'Is that your bus up there?'

The man chuckled. 'I am an orchestra conductor! And I have brought all my orchestra on vacation.' Just then a loud trumpeting noise came from inside the bus.

'Are they playing their instruments?' asked Kilkenny. The Great Conductor went rather red.

'No, they're all snoring. I can't find any new tunes for them to play, so they've locked themselves in the bus, and refuse to wake up.'

It just so happens, that the orchestra bus had parked in a field full of animals. And they had all gathered round when they heard the snoring. This gave Kilkenny a great idea.

First he whispered to the donkeys, then to the pigs, then to the goats and the dairy cows. The Great Conductor looked puzzled. 'All together now,' cried Kilkenny. 'One, two, three, . . .'

What a din! It echoed across the fields, three times round the mountains and back again. The orchestra jumped out of their seats and came tumbling out of the bus.

The Great Conductor laughed so much he almost fell into the tuba. 'I'll play you some new tunes on my flute,' said Kilkenny to the orchestra. 'That is, if I can stop laughing.'

So Kilkenny played the best tunes he knew. And when the orchestra heard such lovely music played by a cat on a flute, they felt quite ashamed for sitting snoring in their bus.

Kilkenny's Mistress made some cupcakes, and they all had a picnic on the grass. 'We must start rehearsing straight away,' said the Great Conductor, 'and Kilkenny must play his flute.'

'You can't play dressed like that,' said Kilkenny's Master with a grin. 'Where are your vacation clothes?'

'Whooppee,' yelled the whole orchestra, and they changed into their shorts and tee-shirts. They grabbed their instruments and ran on to the beach. Kilkenny played his flute and the orchestra joined in . . . it sounded beautiful.

They played together on the beach every day for two weeks. Until at last the Great Conductor told them it was time to go back home. The orchestra felt very sad.

That night the Great Conductor went to Kilkenny's cottage. 'Will you let Kilkenny come back with us and play his flute in a concert?' he begged the cat's Master.

So Kilkenny gave his first concert. No one had ever seen a cat that played the flute before. The audience was thrilled. They clapped and cheered and sent him bunches of flowers.

Every day people lined up to buy tickets for his concerts. They arrived at the concert hall early in the morning and waited all day. Sometimes the line

stretched twice round the concert hall, right down the street and up the other side. And they all came to hear the cat that played the flute.

Every night Kilkenny would telephone his Master to tell him about the concert. His Master sounded very sad because he missed his cat so much.

'It's time I went back home,' Kilkenny decided.

'Please play your tunes just once more,' said the Great Conductor, and he gave the orchestra a big wink.

So Kilkenny was taken into a big empty room. The Great Conductor sat outside and peered at him through a window. 'How strange,' thought Kilkenny. 'Here I am playing to nobody!'

Next day it was time to say goodbye. The Great Conductor smiled at Kilkenny. 'Here is your very own record – you made it yesterday.' And he gave him lots of copies.

Back at home Kilkenny often plays his record and every year the whole orchestra, the Great Conductor and Kilkenny get together and make beautiful music.